A Bench on Which to Rest

A Bench on

The Diary of an Emigrant

Elena Maccaferri

Which to Rest

A NOVEL

Translated from the Italian by MARIA COLFER PHILLIPS

HERODIAS NEW YORK LONDON

Originally published in Italy under the title *Diario di una emigrante*, 1976.

Published by HERODIAS, INC.
346 First Avenue, New York, NY 10009
HERODIAS, LTD.
24 Lacy Road, London, SW15 1NL

Manufactured in the United States of America
Design by Charles B. Hames

LIBRARY OF CONGRESS CATALOGING-IN-PUBLICATION DATA

Maccaferri, Elena, 1921–1977.
   [Diario di una emigrante. English]
   A bench on which to rest : the diary of an emigrant : a novel /
Elena Maccaferri ; translated from the Italian by Maria Colfer Phillips.
      p. cm.
   ISBN 1–928746–02–0
   I. Phillips, Maria Colfer, 1966–   . II. Title.
PQ4873.A185D5313   1999
853'.914—dc21   99–32971
                                     CIP

BRITISH LIBRARY CATALOGUING IN PUBLICATION DATA

A catalogue record of this book is available
from the British Library.

ISBN 1–928746–02–0

10 9 8 7 6 5 4 3 2 1

First Edition 1999

Dedicated to "Paraviere"

I WAS BORN near a place called Paraviere, a small, unknown part of the Apennine hills, with a few houses and a Catholic church. Three valleys away from my home and next to the church was an elementary school that went up to the fifth grade. Closer to us was the ancient Monteveglio Abbey on the brow of a slope with a tiny cemetery next to it, in ruins. We attended mass at the Abbey since there weren't any large gullies to cross and because many of our dear departed were buried there.

I only made it to the third grade and repeated it three times. Then I was dismissed because I wasn't allowed to repeat it again. It's not that I didn't like to study, but we lived very far from the school. I was the eldest of four siblings and Mama wasn't in the greatest of health, so I went to school when I could. Naturally, when I didn't go to school I helped Mama at home, took care of the little ones and helped Papa in the stable. I remember times sitting on a boulder overlooking the valley when I would have left gladly, over the hills, towards the great sky-filled horizon. I felt this way often in the winter.

In the summer, however, I was very happy. My happiness started with the cherry blossoms, and it continued with the flowers and fruits until the leaves of life turned red. It started with the swallows that flew around and around the barnyard, as they slipped under the eaves, and made their way back to the sky. In the fall we gathered many dead ones from the fields. It was very sad.

Papa owned the farm. I thought it was a beautiful farm, even though it was tiresome and Papa dreamed of flat lands far, far away, beyond the valleys. We all worked on the hills in the summer. Even my aunts came to work, but I couldn't stay with them in the fields under the sun collecting the hay, grain and potatoes. I helped Mama and brought the wine and food to those who worked. In the evening I shucked the grain left cut in the fields and I can still feel my skin sting from the scratches of the grain stalks.

In the summer everyone was happy. Papa always hoped for the best harvest. In the winter he would realize that it was never any better than any of the previous years' harvests.

We all loved our land, and we children also loved the slopes that surrounded it. The hills were our playground. When we brought our fourteen lambs out to graze on the slopes, we would run up and down, feeling the rolling stones, sand, and rocks under our feet. When the trellises overflowed with flowers, their scent filled us with extraordinary joy and we would slide from plant to plant, from tuft to tuft, trying to cling to that scent.

Our farm was on the top of a hill and we could see the other farm houses around us. It was as though we were always looking into other peoples' lives. We knew when they did the laundry, when they woke up, and when they slept.

We had only four cows, so we rented the neighbor's oxen to do the plowing. In those times, plowing was like a soft and monotonous chant. A chorus of voices would reach us up there at dawn and incite the animals up the steep slopes. The congregations of cows were spread out here and there through the hills like a nativity scene.

Our house was made of stone with the silo dividing it from the barn. Mama kept the house very clean and in order. When you entered it you would smell the many good smells that made you feel secure: the smell of clean laundry, baked bread barely out of the oven, burned wood, and home-made soap.

In the winter the wind blew hard, but in the summer you could stay cool and it even felt like there was a little air from paradise up there.

For two years I went to school alone, then my sister Edmea started to come with me. We had fun together and we would take all the shortcuts we could through the hills. I would help her up and down by holding her tight by the strap of her book bag. The school teacher, who was from the city, would always say; 'Can't you come to school with a little less mud on your shoes?', and then she would smile. She knew that rural children lived with dirt inside and outside their home. On the way back from school we would take the steep road instead—which wasn't as challenging—and where we had the best chance of meeting a carriage that could give us a lift.

Papa wasn't very religious and didn't go to mass. Mama, on the other hand, was very religious. Her biggest regret was not being closer to the Parish and not being able to go more often. She could get to the Abbey faster along the crest of the hills, and sometimes during the week, she would leave early in the morning and return serene with her hair full of wind and color in her face—giving us all the impression that she had just come back from heaven. As a young girl she was a Daughter of Mary. She had participated in all the processions of her parish with the white robe and blue sash that she kept in a drawer with a picture of Padre Pio, a few sacred medallions, and a few discolored rose petals from Santa Rita. She even taught the Catechism in the parish, and as a result, we knew many things about God that others didn't. We never disappointed Mama in religion class at school.

We were convinced that Mama was once a very important person in her village. When we visited her family six valleys away once a year, they would always talk about the Procession and of the rice cake that was dessert on religious holidays. They were all very religious in Mama's house and two of our cousins were in the Seminary and they talked about their future with high regard. In Papa's house, instead, they never talked about religion, although they all respected the education our mother had given us. I knew that Mama wished with all the strength of her faith that Padre Pio would grant her the miracle of converting Papa to religious practice.

I remember we were already fairly grown up when Mama was able to realize her dream of going to San Giovanni Rotondo. To us it seemed like she was leaving for a trip to Eternity. Even Papa was very anxious. One of my aunts came to take care of the house during her absence, but to us it seemed as if Mama had abandoned us forever. We were scared when even Papa felt it—even though he wouldn't admit it. Instead, he would pretend to be indifferent to the infinite kilometers that she would cross in her pilgrimage.

Papa had been to Bologna maybe five times in his life and the same to Florence. His trips were mostly limited to the markets of Vignola and Bazzano for cherries and calves. We children had never been to Bologna or Florence, and we knew little of cities except for the rare city slicker who drove by in a marvelous automobile on the big road far away.

Finally Mama returned, more a saint than ever, with the certainty that my father would convert himself to religious sentiment since

Father Pio had so assured her. She came home with many little medallions and saintly memorabilia for us, the family, and the neighbors. She talked and talked until late at night, even though she showed signs of wear and emotional exhaustion from her trip. Papa was too happy not to accept the medallion she put around his neck, but I think he was jealous of the fact that his wife had made such a lady's trip by bus and had stayed in a hotel. We were enchanted by everything she had to tell us. The bus was lavish, the hotels were castles, and Father Pio was a real saint.

For three days my mother felt as if she were still on the bus and stayed pale and tired; and to us she seemed a little like a saint herself. She then regained her strength and our lives returned to normal in the wind and sun.

Bruno and Torquato, my two younger brothers, started to go to school when I stopped. I would watch them leave early in the morning with Edmea and I would feel like crying. I had to help Mama and Papa since, on those hills, even an extra set of young hands was precious.

The most important events of our lives continued to be the births of the calves and the harvests. Among the episodes that remained fiercely imprinted in my memory was when two calves died, and when a cow swelled up and survived. It was a quick tragedy for the calves, but for the cow we held a prayer vigil while Papa led her around in circles tirelessly all night. The beast was panting and drooling with teary eyes, as if from crying; it seemed as though she was asking us to let her die. Neighbors came and each one offered advice. A shaman, said to have magical powers, even came to 'give her the sign.' Mama lit a candle to Saint Anthony, protector of animals.

When the cow knelt down, everyone hastened to pick her up, but she fell bit by bit until she was rolling on the ground, her stomach as big as a mountain. Then my father did something horrible. In desperation he grabbed a pitchfork and thrust it into the cow's belly. I ran away screaming followed by my little brothers. We hid under a bush, where, crying and holding on to each other, we fell asleep. Many hours had passed by the time my mother found us and reassured us that the cow was alive. She hugged us and told us that Saint Anthony had made a miracle happen. The veterinarian even came in the afternoon, but he left right away without asking for his fee since he didn't heal the cow. The shaman spent the whole day with us and stayed for supper. It seemed that he had saved the cow, but Mama said it was Saint Anthony who saved her. We would never forget Papa's extreme violence in dealing with the cow's illness.

I was already a young woman of twenty. From the window of our house on the hill, I started following the love life of my peers. Many had already been engaged for many years. I didn't have anyone. My parents were very strict and they never let me go to dances in the village or to the dairy during the harvest season. We were, as I already knew, very poor. I was neither pretty, exuberant, nor talkative. I felt myself aging without feeling like a woman. Though I did know I was a good woman. I was as able as a man in the fields. At home I knew how to do everything: sew, cook, clean, make bread, knit, spin wool and hemp, but no one showed up on our hill or in my heart. At the Parish I was the worst-dressed woman and the men would look only at the other girls. After church, with great haste, I would take the road back home without a look or a compliment to follow me.

It's not that I was terribly affected by this. I knew that Mama and Papa still needed me and wanted a son-in-law in the house. I would have preferred a rich peasant, possibly from the plain where Papa said the harvests were always good; but at the same time I was proud of the position I held in our house. So I really wouldn't have known what to say to a man, yes or no, and I preferred dreaming about the impossible peasant from the plain. The first of my peers to marry were two young girls that lived in the farmhouses under us. They had a wonderful wedding. I don't remember ever having eaten as much in my life. Papa said it was a useless waste of money, and that if I were to marry, he would not have such a big wedding.

Two other young girls who, in the winter, went to work in town married two men from the city. Then there was the unfortunate story of Carmela, who bore a child and was forced to leave her home. Mama said that these things happen to girls who go to work in the city. But I knew they also happen out in the country; only in the country people are honest and marry the woman, whereas city people are sinful and dishonest.

It was like that even for my sister Edmea and Sandro. She told me so. They were wed immediately. Papa didn't have a big wedding since Sandro was poor. Sandro came to live with us. He was a good and strong worker, and the harvest improved with his help.

Even my brothers had grown up. Bruno got tuberculosis and went to the sanitarium. The other was still young, so I was left to work in the fields and the work never let up. Nonetheless, in the winter, while Edmea took care of the house with Mama, I had time to work on my trousseau which one customarily started as a child. There was a large celebration when Giuseppe, Edmea's son was born. I was named godmother.

I kept aging—I was already twenty-seven and no one had knocked on the door to my heart, although I knew I would make a good wife. My name is Climene and I think it's a pretty name, a romantic name. Up until then, however, it hadn't brought me any luck.

I was nearing my twenty-eighth birthday when I heard about Adelmo Toschi. The Toschis were the owners of the Valletta farm, three valleys to the north. They were also the caretakers of the game reserve belonging to the Duke. They were considered people of a class higher than the peasants. Mr. Toschi had been the personal butler to the old Duke. Even the eldest son, Adelmo, took his turn in serving the Duke. Then, a fortunate turn brought Adelmo to America, to a city named Montreal. Adelmo had been there three years and said he had made his fortune. Now he was coming home. He was coming to look for a wife. In the valleys and on the hills there was a lot of talk from house to house. The girls were anxious . . . but I never thought I would be the chosen one.

As is customary with emigrant workers, Adelmo Toschi chose to marry in his country of origin. Also following custom, he asked his parents to find the woman. Pretty if possible, good and capable above all else.

The emigrant has a hard and lonely life. A woman becomes his world, a rock on which to base his life, an outlet for the spirit and the body, an aide, a comfort, an encouragement, the principal goal of his status as an emigrant.

It would only stand to reason that such a rock should be strong and should not crumble. So, pretty, yes, wrote Adelmo, possibly; strong, serious and capable above all else.

The Toschis, the father and mother, invited my parents and spoke clearly. I think Papa and Mama were more excited about the fortune that would fall to them more than anything else. The Toschis were financially well-off and were recognized for their great integrity. Adelmo was American. All this meant a lot of money and good social standing. My parents then told me what was proposed to them. I was left speechless. In all our poverty, and in the humility of my little education, it seemed like a miracle from Saint Anthony.

The Abyssinian war was approaching during that time and many women watched their husbands and fiancés leave as they were called to arms. Those who didn't have either would wallow in the idea of marriage. In the country, a girl who doesn't get married is like a tree that doesn't bear fruit. She becomes the person who dwells on the events of those who are married. I had already prepared myself for such a destiny, but as luck would have it, a whole new wonderful world was opening up before me.

I remember afterwards, when word got out that I was the candidate, everyone who lost out took to telling strange stories about Adelmo Toschi. They said he was a tyrannical boy who never took things seriously. This gossip bothered Mama, but Papa said that those who are lucky always have others who envy them. Hadn't Adelmo made money in America? Wasn't this proof of his love of work? Hadn't he become a skilled worker? He came to find a woman in Italy just as someone with serious intentions would, and above all, he had his parents pick her out. And what about the letters he wrote? Weren't they from a person with feelings and principles?

"The women . . .", Mama would say timidly.

"Better now than later," Papa would say.

My mother still held on to her doubts until Adelmo's arrival. Any mother or father in my homeland would have been infinitely proud of such a son-in-law. The Parish Priest showed us Canada on his map which didn't seem too far away since the map was small.

"At least you'll have water," Papa said when the Parish Priest showed us how much water there was in Canada. Our well was so dry we often had to take barrels and go to other farms or valleys to fetch more. The Parish Priest also said there were many convents and churches in Montreal. "They are people who have the fear of God in them," said Mama with a sigh of relief.

Adelmo came from Canada on a 'transatlantic', and to our town he rode a flaming-red motorcycle. Word went through the hills and valleys right away. I saw him a few days later, but I knew of his arrival and I stayed awake nights with the happiness and anticipation of our meeting. Papa and Mama met him before I did and they both agreed once again that they were lucky.

ELENA MACCAFERRI

"A real gentleman, Climene," said Papa. "handsome, strong and with money. He's coming to meet you tomorrow so you can speak together. I think you'll be very fortunate to have him."

"I think so too," said Mama, "even though the thought of your going so far away breaks my heart."

From behind the curtains in my room I watched the little road that wound its way down through the hills, into the valley, towards the big road. I had been waiting for Adelmo for two hours. I spent a long time doing my hair. I had so much and such long hair that I put it up in a large bun. I was wearing my Sunday dress and had sprayed my wrists and hair with Expecting Love, a perfume given to me a long time ago by a relative who worked in a perfume factory. It wasn't a very strong perfume, so when I saw Adelmo's motorcycle appear, I sprayed a little more on my wrists.

I followed the progress of the motorcycle, while inside I felt myself dying from joy and fear. Not one motorcycle, including the veterinarian's, had ever been able to climb the last incline to our house, but Adelmo's made it to the top sliding and snorting.

I saw Papa go to greet him, then Mama came out of the house. My brother Torquato stayed outside to admire the motorcycle while the others went inside. I heard Edmea call me, but I was shaking so badly I could hardly stand, and I didn't have the courage to go downstairs. Edmea came up and stared at me in surprise.

"I'm scared," I told her, shaking all over.

"Don't be silly," said Edmea as she pushed me toward the stairs. I started down the stairs—I can still recall the pain and the joy . . .

I could hear his strong, loud voice along with the voices of Papa and Mama. When I entered the room, Adelmo and Papa were sitting at the table, and Mama was standing with a bottle of wine in her hand. Adelmo got up so fast that I had to force myself not to run away.

Adelmo was more handsome and stronger than I remembered. He came towards me and said: "Do you remember me?"

"At the gully," I said.

As children, we often met in the gullies. Adelmo took my hand and squeezed it hard between his. I didn't have the courage to look at him.

"You don't wear your hair in braids any-more," said Adelmo, and laughed. Papa told me to sit with them. I felt very important since women never sat with the men.

Adelmo talked a lot, sure of himself. He spoke of the ocean as if he knew it better than our river Ghiaia. He said that in his American city there was a much larger river like the ocean and he laughed at our river. He said many wonderful things. He had an automobile the length of three cows. He obviously earned a lot of money. He wore a synthetic shirt; Mama went to touch it and said it was better than silk. Adelmo told Papa he would send him one. He wore a green tie with wild horses on it. Torquato said it was the most beautiful tie he had ever seen, and Adelmo promised to give it to him before he left.

That day we talked. Adelmo would look at me every once in a while as if he were studying a purchase he was about to make, then he would give a brief, warm smile. Before he left he asked Papa if I could go out with him the next day. He agreed.

We went out together constantly for ten days with Sandro or Edmea or Torquato to visit people. In the evening he would come up and we would walk around the house, sit on the rocks, and he would tell me about America and of the wonders it would do for our lives. The first few days I didn't have the courage to speak; then, bit by bit, I built up my confidence as we became friends. I'd never known anyone so strong and so different.

We had a big engagement dinner thrown by the Toschis so Papa carted down three of our best barrels of wine. Everyone said the engagement was better than a wedding. The guests ate and drank without end, and left wandering about in happiness. I was living my greatest dream. I felt I had loved Adelmo for years and that the world was made up only of him.

That night, after the party was over, he walked me home across the hills and valleys, and I took off my shoes so I could walk better.

"Let's go up by the ravine," I said.

"Like we used to," said Adelmo.

He took off his tie and jacket and gave me his hand. We looked at the ridges of the gullies, pure and white in the night like crescents of the moon.

"They're high," said Adelmo, "and steep."

"You don't remember them?" I asked.

"I could never forget them," he said.

"The trees are in bloom," I said.

"They will smell good," he said and he egged me on.

We started to climb and slide and soon we were out of breath. Rocks and sand moved under our feet, and at one point we even slid backwards; but not too far since we were able to grab on to shrubs as we held each other. At one point, Adelmo stopped and took off his shoes as well.

"The rocks feel good under my feet," he said.

We started once again for the top. The ridge was right in front of us but we could easily fall back down trying to reach it. Adelmo let go of me to find a better approach, but he couldn't find one. I supported myself as best I could while trying to hold on to Adelmo who was looking for a good hold to help pull himself up.

"I think . . ." he said as he tried to heave himself upward. I could feel him falling back on me and we started to slide rapidly down the ridge. I helped my descent by sliding, so I wouldn't lose my balance and roll backwards. At the same time I searched for something to grab on to with my hands. Then I felt myself being stopped by Adelmo's arm. He had found something to grasp. He held me tightly until I could find a solid foothold. We had never been this close, and we were out of breath and happy. The flowers had such a wonderful scent.

We started to climb again along the ridge, and this time, Adelmo was able to lift himself and then help me up. We found ourselves in a green pasture that caressed our feet. We stared down the slope of the gully; the white ridges followed one another and disappeared in the dark valley.

"We didn't forget," I said.

"You can't forget," said Adelmo, and he put an arm around my waist and guided me towards a slight dip in the pasture.

We sat next to each other and Adelmo came close and kissed me and told me wonderful things, things I didn't think a man could say to a woman. I pulled him closer to me, and I felt like I was hot earth and the rocks and grass and trees and stars were all in my eyes. And the smell of blossoms mixed with that of the grasses . . .

Almost in answer to my thoughts, Adelmo
fell back to my side and said,

"You are made of good earth."

I remember we stopped talking then and
lay back staring at the stars and a small slice of
the moon in the sky, hand in hand, eyes wide,
with the great hills around us reaching far and
wide. Then Adelmo said, "We'll come back
here to die."

I didn't understand him. I couldn't understand why he was talking about death when I
felt so alive.

We didn't get married in the town since
Adelmo had to leave in a hurry. He said there
was a danger that he would be called to war in
Abyssinia and that would mean the end of his
life in America.

He left without warning, and with the help
of the Parish Priest, I made the necessary
preparations to join him.

I was crazy about Adelmo and all I could do
was cry because the paperwork was taking so
long. Mama cried because I was going far away.

Papa tried to be a little stronger. Torquato envied me. Edmea didn't. She said she wouldn't leave her land for any man even if she was poor and had to work all the time.

I felt bad for Mama's tears, but I was crazy about Adelmo. I think I forgot my love for my mother, my father, my brothers and my land during that time, but I never admitted it.

The paperwork took a long time, so long that I was scared they would soon realize I was expecting a child. I had morning sickness and had to make an effort to hide it from my parents. I wasn't surprised when I found out about it. I knew from that night under the stars that I would be expecting Adelmo's child. I loved the discomfort that was my child with the same intensity that I loved Adelmo. I didn't write to Adelmo about it. I didn't trust the postman since people said he read the letters. He always happened to know everything. I would surprise Adelmo. We rarely wrote regarding other matters. The letters would take very long to arrive, and sometimes I thought they would never arrive.

When I finally received my visa and started to make definite plans for my departure, Adelmo stopped writing. It seemed logical to me, and I reassured Mama who became worried about it.

"I'll meet him in Montreal, at the train station. 'Don't leave the station;' it says so in every letter," and I showed it to her.

The excitement of the last moments of preparation took away any other preoccupation. On top of it all, my brother Bruno, at the sanitarium, got worse. Mama would only go to see him every two months since the trip cost so much. Now she went every fifteen days. She would return with her heart and body aching. I went to see Bruno before I left.

"Are you the one leaving for America?" the nurse asked.

"Yes," I said.

"Then say your good-byes," she said, "because you won't be seeing him again."

So I gathered all my strength with Bruno. I never thought that going away would mean never seeing someone again. Bruno was pale and thin and breathed with difficulty. I asked him what he wanted from Canada—that I would send it to him.

"My health," he said and laughed bitterly. Then he added that he wanted me to send some money so he could rent a car and go see his land again.

"I'll send you some money," I promised and hugged him. When I left, I was crying so hard and felt such pain inside me, I thought I would lose the child I was carrying.

The next day I told Papa and Mama that bringing the trousseau with me would be another unaffordable expense, and that I wanted to sell it to a rich bride. There were sheets and towels and many clothes made of strong hemp. The money I would get for it I would leave to Bruno.

Mama embraced me and cried and even Papa's tired eyes filled with tears. "We'll give him a nice funeral and find him a good grave," he said. The night before I left, Papa said the rosary with us—Mama cried and had a hard time reciting parts of it. So Edmea said, "She's going to get married, to make a good life for herself. We should be happy. And if it doesn't work out, we'll always be here."

"All animals know the road home," said Papa.

Mama felt better and we drank some wine; I wanted to be with Adelmo and end this torture of leaving that was bringing me down like a drowning hand. The next day I had already forgotten the pain of that moment. My farewell with Mama was agonizing mostly for her. Once again, I didn't have any awareness of the world around me, of the distance, of the love of a mother, of what others felt. I was once again and above all else, crazy about Adelmo.

Papa took me to Genova. With the cows, we took the cart down to the main road to help with all my belongings. I don't know why, but I noticed every stone and every blade of grass on that road which I knew so well. Torquato, who was leading the cows, waited for us to get the luggage and I can still picture him leaning on the yoke, kind and patient like his cows.

We waited in Bologna for the train to Genova while eating some of the sandwiches Mama had made for us. Papa kept the suitcase between his legs whether in the station or on the train. We were very worried about losing the one suitcase that contained everything I owned.

There was so much confusion at the port, that the sound of the band that was playing got lost. There were people yelling, crying and laughing. I had never seen the ocean or a ship. I felt sick, but I think it was because of Adelmo's child that I was carrying away with me—on that ocean and on that ship. Then someone bumped into me and I grabbed Papa and told him I would go up to the deck to wave good-bye to him from there.

"Don't lose the suitcase," he said, "it's like your home."

I reassured him I wouldn't, then, with his help, I loaded the suitcase on my shoulder and the other packages in my free hand. Dizzily, I found my way to the end of a line of people who were boarding the ship. I then tried to find my way to a deck where I could see my father. After searching and asking people, I finally let go of my heavy burden of a suitcase, placed it between my feet, and stood at the rail. There was a sea of people, and then I saw him and he saw me and we stared at each other, I above, he below, for more than an hour.

The ship blew it's whistle and started to get under way. The music and shouts and groans of the people were frightening me. I started to wave furiously, but I don't know if my father saw me. Leaning against a column, in a corner by himself, he was sobbing into a big white handkerchief. I stayed at the rail until the ship changed direction and he was hidden from me. I promptly forgot the suitcase and ran along the decks filled with emigrants, crying out my parents' names and trying to still keep sight of my father. I thought I would go crazy from the pain, and I kept yelling louder and louder until someone grabbed me by the arm.

"What's the matter?" He was an officer, or so I thought. I got scared. "The suitcase," I said. In saying this I realized that I had forgotten the suitcase. I left the officer and ran back to the deck. The suitcase was there all by itself, since all the people had moved to the decks facing the pier.

'It's like your home,' father had said and I sat on that nothing house of mine and started crying softly and felt like the loneliest person in the world. Then I thought of Adelmo's child and I caressed him and a feeling of tenderness comforted me. I looked around. There was a strange silence. No more music or yelling. The deck was deserted. I looked at my new surroundings—the banners, the immense smoke stacks, the life boats.

"Where am I going?" I asked myself. "My child will be born a Canadian," I told myself.

I faced the water. It was black because there wasn't any sun. Land was already far away. My thoughts ran to the Apennine hills and valleys. Again my eyes filled with tears. I wondered if my father was still crying. I thought of my mother who was probably praying, 'Why is there an ocean? An America?'

I looked up. On the deck above me three people were talking and laughing. They were elegant people from first class. I placed my hands together on my womb and said intensely, "I will work hard, hard, with Adelmo and I will return in first class and you will be privileged." I said it seriously and with all my will. I then felt stronger, picked myself up, grabbed the suitcase, and slowly hauled it through the maze of corridors full of people.

There were four people in my cabin. There was an Italian-American bride who had come to Italy to find her relatives. She knew a lot about ships and taught us many things. There was an old lady who was going to join her children in Toronto. The third woman was going to Montreal, her name was Catina. They were all from the south of Italy and older than I. The bride wore gaudy clothes and a lot of fake jewelry. The old lady and Catina always wore black. When the bride was gone, the old lady would take off her shoes since she wasn't used to wearing any. She had a sad and lost look about her and she always had a Rosary in her hands. Catina was chubby, happy, and affectionate. She was going to join her brother who had a large family of eight.

We became close. Maybe it was because she was going to Montreal, or maybe because she spoke a clearer Italian. I told her about Adelmo; she told me about her home and of all her relatives, alive and dead, all round the world. In the dining room, in the evenings, I would sit next to her and we would listen to the music and watch the others dance. There

were a lot of children—many young emigrants. I would refuse to dance, but Catina
always accepted and really enjoyed herself. I
was a little scared when she wasn't near me.
Catina was happy to join her brother whom
she loved very much. She was happy to know
that even with all those people in the house,
she was needed.

We had rough seas and the old lady and the
bride vomited for days. The old lady was crying and kept saying something that Catina
translated for me as 'Mother of God, save us
from this sinking ship!' Catina would reassure
her. I tried to get the old woman to eat something for fear she would die of starvation.
Deep down I was scared of sinking also, and I
kept thinking I might not see Adelmo or my
parents ever again.

Not once during the whole trip did I ever
want to go back. I was madly in love with
Adelmo; he was my life, my child's life, and
everything in my future. Before landing in

Halifax I sent a telegram to Adelmo as we had agreed. Catina had helped me write it, and at the end I put only: 'We are arriving,' since anyone could read the telegram. At the end Catina suggested "Your love," but I told her I was embarrassed, and she then said simply "Climene" would do and would cost less as well.

*I*N HALIFAX, we sat along benches on the quay until we were asked to show our papers. All I heard was the sound of crying children. Then we were herded on to a long train which we rode for what seemed an infinite distance. I was very dizzy, and having been sitting for hours with packages and suitcases all around me, I started feeling ill. Nonetheless, before arriving in Montreal, I was able to change my dress so Adelmo would see me at my best.

The arrival in Montreal was chaotic. I saw my friend Catina embraced by a great number of people. I saw people, people, people, but I didn't see Adelmo.

The station emptied out, then filled again with other people, and emptied out again. During the night, I napped a little on a bench with the suitcase still between my feet. I woke with a start when someone touched my arm. It wasn't Adelmo. It was, it seemed, some railway worker who spoke to me in the unknown language of that place. I tried to explain to him that I was waiting for Adelmo. He left without understanding. I was very tired and my bones ached. I thought of Adelmo, of the warmth of a bed and his body for me and our child. The same worker came back in the morning. Giving up conversation, he signaled for me to follow him. I thought of the suitcase and said no. He left and returned soon after with a cup of hot coffee. I thanked him and drank it all at once. I then understood that he wanted to see my documents, so I showed them to him. He then motioned for me to follow him once again, but I tried to explain to him that I was waiting for Adelmo and would not move from the bench. He left.

The station got busy again. Faces changed, but the station and the benches stayed the same—inhospitable. The worker returned with a gentleman who spoke to me in Italian. He said he worked for the Consul and wanted to know what I was doing at the station. I told him I was awaiting my fiancé Adelmo Toschi. He looked at me with a strange air and said, "You can't just stay in the station."

"But he said to wait here."

"Do you have any money?"

"A little. I have to get married."

He looked disconcerted. "Come to the Consulate." he said, "We'll find your Adelmo."

"I can't," I said, "I have to wait."

"Do you have his home address?"

"Yes," I said, and I looked through my purse.

He took it. "Come to the Consulate," he repeated. "We'll see what we can do."

"No." I said. "He told me to wait for him here." The two of them spoke in some strange language, then the gentlemen turned to me again.

"Do you have money to eat?"

"Yes."

"Italian money?"

"Yes."

He took two dollars from his pocket and gave them to me. "If you are hungry there is a place over there where you can find something to eat. In the meantime, I'll look for your Adelmo. I'll meet you here."

He never came back. That afternoon, an Italian priest came with a lady. The priest told me, "Come with me. I found a place for you to sleep tonight at a convent."

I told him I was waiting for Adelmo.

"I know," he said. "They called me from the Consulate. We have news of your Adelmo, but let's get out of here so we can talk about it. We'll be more comfortable at the Parish."

So I followed him because he knew about Adelmo. The lady rode in the taxi with us and we traveled for a long time. There was so much traffic that I often had to close my eyes for fear.

"It's a big country," I said. The priest was sitting in the front next to the driver. Perhaps he didn't hear me. The woman said nothing. I wondered what language she spoke. I then understood she was Italian. Then, in Italian, she told me Adelmo had been in her boarding house and that he had married an Italian-Canadian a month ago and had left for Vancouver, a place as far as Italy but still in the same country.

"I don't believe it," I said. Then the priest showed me the marriage certificate since Adelmo had been married in his church. I couldn't even cry.

"There are many other good immigrants," said the priest encouragingly. But I wanted Adelmo, the father of my child. "Adelmo was unfortunate," said the lady.

"And me?" I said.

"You too," said the lady, "you too are unfortunate, but not all the unfortunate ones come here and get hurt."

"Why did he get married? Why didn't he tell me?"

The priest got out and the lady told me the Italian-Canadian girl was expecting a child and Adelmo had to do his duty.

"And me?"

"Adelmo did his duty even though he was waiting and wanting you. Let's hope they are happy."

"And me?"

"The sisters will take care of you. I understand it's a hard blow for you, but nothing that can't be fixed. There are so many good immigrants without women, and in this country they make a good living. But if you want, we could always try to repatriate you."

"Go home?"

"If you want." I remember I rose to my feet. All of a sudden everything I had been told became perfectly clear. It was clear that everything was irrevocable: Adelmo, my child, my home. It seemed there was no place in the world for me or my child, and as I was trying to take a breath into my empty lungs, a loud yell began to build and build from the bottom of my soul. The lady ran to me and took me in her arms. The priest came in at once, but I had already regained my composure.

"Excuse me," I said, and I went to leave.

"Where are you going?" asked the priest and the lady. I looked at her in a stupor. 'Where was I going?' The priest turned to the woman.

"It would be a good idea to bring her to the sisters. She'll calm down there."

"I have a friend."

"Where?"

"Here, in Montreal." I looked in my purse for the address of my traveling companion, the only person who was a link between the land I had left and the one to which I had come.

They looked at the address. "I'll take her," said the lady, "and if she can't make arrangements there, I'll bring her to the Sisters."

They were celebrating Catina's arrival at the Ciacchi home. Everyone was at the dinner table. There were so many people that it made me tired watching Catina among all those faces, happy and red with food and wine. Catina ran to me in surprise.

"Adelmo wasn't there," I said. "He got married." The lady who was with me went to speak. "Come, come," said Catina, "I'll take care of it, madam. Leave her with me. She's like my sister."

So I found myself sitting at the table next to Catina in the midst of all those people who had come to celebrate my arrival as well, just as if I were Catina's sister. I understood little of what they were saying because they were speaking in their dialect, but I understood that they were happy I was with them, and that they cared about me and wanted me to be happy like them. So I ate and drank everything they offered me. And I laughed . . . I sang and laughed and dried my tears from laughing so hard until I felt sick and had to go to bed.

When I woke the next morning, I found a razor blade and I slit my wrists because I wanted to die. When I saw the blood and knew I was taking it away from my child and Adelmo's child, I started yelling. The whole family came in, but Catina and her brother Ciccio led them out of the room. They bandaged my wrists and the blood stopped flowing. They gave me a bit of brandy and sat in front of me and I told Catina and Ciccio that I was expecting Adelmo's child. Catina started crying, but Ciccio said: "There's a solution for everything."

They found me a full-time housekeeping job where I stayed for a few months. During that time, the Toschis and my mother, who had learned of Adelmo's wedding, wrote to the Consulate often and with despair for news about me. The Consulate called on me several times, but I didn't want to read the letters. Then one day the Consul himself came.

"Listen, young lady, try to write to your parents. All we're doing is writing letters. Tell them you have a good job as a housekeeper. I don't know how to tell them anymore. The Marshal wrote, the Parish Priest wrote, we answered everyone. You're breaking your mother's heart. You're in good health, exuberant, you have a good job. Things didn't go well with your fiancé? You'll find another, but you have to write. You have to calm them down. We gave them everything we have—that Adelmo Toschi was definitely married and in Vancouver, and that you are here working. But they don't want to believe us. Here, this bundle of letters is yours."

I looked at the package that was filled with Mama's tears. I took them, squeezed them as I would my mother, and wearily got to my feet. The Consul gave me a long look and I reddened and lowered my head.

"Don't tell me that . . ." he said. I nodded without looking at him.

"Does your mother know?"

"No."

"What are you going to do?"

"I don't know."

"Will he marry you?"

"Who?"

"Him." I shook my head.

"Great!" thundered the Consul, "What a mess! And such a wise face! Is this why you don't write? Did you come here to give birth or work hard?"

"Work hard, Mr. Consul, sir."

"And now what are you going to do?" I looked at him desperately.

"I don't know, sir, I really don't know!"

"Do you have the means to support it?"

"I don't know . . ."

"Do you understand this is a problem?"

"Yes, Mr. Consul, a big one."

"And when are you going to tell you parents?"

"I'm not going to tell them, sir." He shook his head and gave me a long lecture and finished by saying, "This is a country where you can raise a family, but a country where you have to live in decency. Otherwise you should just go home."

"Yes, sir."

"What you have told me will remain between you and me. But write home, please."

As I was leaving he asked me again, "Do you have someone to talk to about this?"

"Yes."

"Let's hope they give you good advice. In any case, I am always here."

"Thank you, sir." He shook his head desolately.

Catina and her brother Ciccio said I had to give up my child. They said that it would have a much better life adopted by a good, rich family that was well-liked and respected. There was no way I could support it. It would be hard for me to find a husband. It would be better for both of us.

I cried the whole night through trying to decide.

Ciccio said he would find me a good husband right away in Italy, and that the others would help me get through it. I decided to go to the Consul before making the decision. "I think it would be best," said the Consul, "especially for the child."

"But I will never see him again."

"You will never see him, but no one will know anything about it, here or in Italy."

"Would you give your son away?" I asked. He shifted in his chair.

"I'm not a woman," he said.

So I went with Catina where they gave me a number and I was no longer Climene, but a number, because my child couldn't know who his mother or father were. So I signed a piece of paper giving up the best part of my life, and when it was done, I felt as if I had torn my insides out and I fell to the ground. They helped me up and told me I could still change my mind, but that I would not be able to see the baby unless I decided to keep it. The decision would become irrevocable a few months after the birth. When I left with Catina I met other numbers, but no one seemed as sad and hurt as I felt.

By the seventh month, I stopped working and went into a clinic where I caressed and adored the child I would never see. Those were a happy two months. I worked in the clinic and supported myself. I had it in my head that Adelmo, the child, and I were living the most marvelous dream, the most impossible dream I could ever have imagined.

I didn't go back on my decision, I didn't see my child, and I didn't know whether it was a boy or a girl. I found myself alone again, without Adelmo or my child. A part of my life had passed, but still I felt it with me in the deepest part of my being, a huge scar made of so much love and pain that only God can know.

I went back to work. I was earning good wages, I made myself a few dresses, and I wrote home more often and started sending them money regularly. My mother calmed down and my father forgave me for my silence. I even wrote to the Toschis because I cared a lot for Adelmo and I thought of them as my second parents.

I heard more news of Adelmo when I again ran into his former landlady. She told me that when it all happened, Adelmo was really desperate because he really loved me; but, she said, he got into a bad situation when he went out with that girl. She repeated that Adelmo loved me very much, that he would carry my letters in his pockets and kiss them in front of everyone and tell them how I would make the best bride in the world. I don't know why she wanted so badly for me to believe that Adelmo loved me so much. I was sure he had loved me—just as I was sure that I had loved him.

Ciccio showed me many pictures of young men from his home town who were eager to emigrate. These men were, for the sake of expediting paperwork and who knows what other reasons, looking for wives. Ciccio was very partial to one of his distant relatives, Beppe, whom he said was kind and good-natured and wasn't at all curious about my past.

"He will never know about your child. As for the rest, well, all women aren't the same. If he ever has any doubts, I'm sure he would never hold it against you." I didn't find him very attractive, to tell the truth, but I trusted Ciccio and besides, a woman needs to marry.

"This way you can regain your reputation and virtue," said Ciccio with satisfaction. I went with Catina to get my picture taken by a friend of Ciccio's who was a good photographer at a reasonable price. He took pictures from the front, back, and side. He took pictures of my whole body, from the waist up only, and of my head. He tried to focus on parts of my body that were the most complimentary. When I saw the pictures I felt a little embarrassed, since they were so different from what I thought I looked like.

Ciccio added different facts about me to the pictures—all good. I was kind, hard working, a good cook, religious, fairly intelligent, but not too independent. I was frugal, very capable in the home, and from the North. The pictures were there to show what I looked like. It looked good, said Ciccio, it really looked good.

Beppe answered that I would suit him. So we were married by proxy, he in Italy, and I in Montreal. I rented a room in the city where I brought my few possessions, a little stove, and two little pots. I bought four sheets and four pillow cases. Catina gave me a pink flannel nightgown, Ciccio gave me some plates, and everyone in the family added something.

Tears overwhelmed me when I had finished arranging my room and gave it a final glance. I sat on the bed with my heart cold and empty. A few days later we went to the train station to get Beppe. He arrived carrying a large suitcase on his strong shoulders. We recognized each other, looked at each other and he gave me his hand.

"Good," he said with a big smile.

"Good," I said with a lump in my throat.

We went to Ciccio's house in two cars. There were already many guests there. There was a big party with music, white flowers, sweets, and champagne. Beppe and I were sitting next to each other, our wrists touching, but we couldn't look each other in the eye.

We walked home since it wasn't far, Beppe with his big suitcase on his shoulders, not talking, not looking at each other.

While I was unpacking his suitcase, he was standing behind me embarrassed. Then I felt his large hand on my shoulder. I turned around and we found ourselves facing each other.

"Why are you crying?" he asked me. I threw myself in his arms, sobbing.

He held me tight against him and softly said, "It's hard to care for another right away."

"Oh!" I moaned.

But Beppe couldn't understand, he didn't know how to help me, nor could he help me.

He stroked my head—hard and mechanically. I regained my composure and shifted.

"I'm sorry," I said.

"It's hard," he repeated.

"I'll try to love you," I said.

"I think I already love you," he said. The goodness of his words softened me.

"You must be a very good person," I said.

"You too," he said.

"We'll be happy together," I said decisively.

"We will," he said.

Then I asked him to turn out the light and I laid on the bed. He undressed and came close to me, and I forced myself with all my will to find the desperate desire in me for my hot earth under my back—and the rocks and grass and trees and stars all in my eyes like that night long ago.

BEPPE STARTED out doing odd jobs since he wasn't skilled in any particular trade and couldn't speak English or French. He washed dishes, gardened, shovelled snow, and ran errands. I kept working as a housekeeper during the day. A year later, Beppe found a full-time job and I was pregnant again. Rosa was born.

The next year Dino was born. I couldn't work anymore since I had to take care of the children. Beppe wasn't earning very much and life was hard. That's when I started thinking of the countryside. There I would be able to work, even with children. I explained my idea to him which he greeted with enthusiasm as always. With the help of one of Ciccio's friends, we were able to get a loan, and we bought a piece of property on the other side of the river with four cows, baby chicks, and two little pigs.

During the first summer, we fixed up the house and barn and worked the land that was still good, black, rich and not depleted. Even though Rosa and Dino were still very small, I worked with all my might to get something from the land so we could maintain ourselves without any other expenses. It was a very difficult summer. When I worked by the river-bank I tied the children to a tree for fear of their running and falling into the depths of the St. Lawrence. Tired, Beppe and I would return home at night. I would fix dinner, Beppe would work on some other chore; then to bed, exhausted. From our bed I could see the open sky over the St. Lawrence, and when there was a full moon, I would stay awake and stare at it with a pain as big and powerful as the universe itself.

On weekends we would organize picnics for Ciccio's friends that always grew in num-ber. I would make tasty, sweet smelling home-made pasta and bread that earned us good money. We even got down to making home-made cheeses that sold faster than we could keep up with.

Beppe was a strong worker, but I was a better organizer. At times he would feel like I was bossing him around, and he would get furious and say that Ciccio had deceived him about my docile nature. But he would calm down right away and apologize, returning to his gentle and affectionate self. Beppe had an extraordinarily kind temperament. I know he couldn't forgive me for being from the North, for speaking better Italian, for working as hard as he did, and knowing how to organize things better; but he never tried to hurt me, when I think he could have. In a certain way, he was even excessively proud of me. He would bore our friends by going on about my talents. He would hold me in bed, next to him, saying the sweetest, most emotional things. I had to keep forcing myself not to compare him to Adelmo, but when he was so tender and sweet, I would give myself over to thinking that Adelmo would never have been capable of so much.

It wasn't really Adelmo *the man* that tormented me. It was as much Adelmo's land as it was my land, my people, my feelings. Beppe wasn't completely wrong in thinking that I was different from him, just as I thought him different from me. His people and family were strange to me, just as mine were to him. It's as if we had come from two different worlds. We couldn't understand each other's dialects either. The things we had most in common were our status as immigrants, our religion, our pasta, and our wine and oil. Even our history separated us. In his land they had the Roman ruins, in our land people talked about the Lombards and Matilde of Canossa. We were both just as ignorant, and in our own hearts we were brought up on such different folk tales, that, because of our ignorance, we could never relate to one another.

Rosa and Dino were growing up well. When weariness would overcome me, I had to force myself to erase the shadow of my other child from them and fight the very sweet and painful affection that I carried for it inside myself. I had to tell myself that it wasn't unfair that Dino and Rosa could be here and not the other. I had to fight not to run and find shelter near the other child in my weariness and melancholy. I say I had to fight because if I were to attach myself to the child, the unknown child, the others, Dino and Rosa—I would become estranged from them and a sense of hatred would consume me. Many times I would yell at them and wonder if it wasn't my hatred guiding me. Beppe would even reproach me for being too hard on the children, and feelings of remorse would then devour me. And yet, I was a perfectly well-balanced and reasonable person; but the huge scar deep inside me would never heal.

Beppe brought a great passion of his to Canada: Fascism. The little bit of time he had to spare he spent on the other side of the river, in the Italian quarter of the city, at the Fascist assemblies. Then he would come home and talk about it, but I was never up on politics. My father was never interested and we were too high up and isolated on the hill to receive any political echoes from the cities or villages. They gave Beppe a responsibility that made him very proud: he carried the pennant. Because of this he was often in newspaper pictures. During that time, Mussolini was well-known even overseas and I felt proud of Beppe. I liked his black shirts more than his white, and we had a large picture of Mussolini in the house—and next to it a pennant with gold fringes.

When talk of war started, our farm was in optimal condition and the price of our products started to rise. We had seventy good cows, five hundred chickens and about twenty pigs. We sold almost everything privately, which gave us a good profit margin. Our own work maintained everything. When I think of those times, I see countless eggs, calves born on stormy winter nights, huge sunsets over the forests across the river, and quiet ships illuminated in the night.

Sometimes I would sit with the children on the front steps of the house, at sunset, that was always beautiful, and I would tell them about the Monteveglio Abbey and of the Emperor's son, of the almond trees in bloom and the tasty peaches. They were very small and it seemed as though I was only telling myself these things. Sometimes Beppe would sit with us and tell us about his vineyard where many Romans were supposed to be buried, since every now and then a piece of a vase or a bronze sculpture would pop up. And how they would have to hurry and bury everything again or the government would take away their vineyard to dig up the ruins.

I continued to send money to my parents with letters that they would read to all the neighbors. I knew they were very proud of us. At that time, my brother Bruno died in the

Sanitarium, Torquato was still in the army, and Edmea had two more children. Work was hard there, but they seemed happy despite Bruno's tragedy and Torquato's absence. Torquato wrote to me that with the money I had sent my father, he was hoping to buy himself and his girlfriend a plot of land on the plain. That way Edmea could keep our land in the hills.

Italy's declaration of war surprised us. I cried the whole night thinking I would never hear from my parents again. Beppe consoled me, saying that we were fortunate to have come from the country. Prices increased some more. I decided to open a bank account in Torquato's name for his land, and I continued to put money into it.

I remember that evening well. I had put the children to bed and was finishing up in the kitchen when they knocked at the door. I went to open it and found myself face to face with two officers. They asked if Beppe were home.

"Yes," said Beppe and he came forward. They said he had to go with them. I said he could go the following day. No, they said right away. And so they took him away and I was left at home alone, at night, for the first time since we were married. I couldn't sleep. I was cold and felt a strange fear. For days I tried to find out where he was and what they wanted from him. When I finally found someone who knew, they said Beppe had carried the pennant at the Fascist assemblies. They would hold him for questioning. So he went to a concentration camp, like Ciccio and many others who were Fascists. No one knew when they would be back.

I found myself alone. I understood that with two children, the cows, the chickens, the pigs, and the land I would never make it. But farmers did well in those days and for a time I tried to survive on my own. The neighbors came to lend a hand. Some took care of the children, some milked the cows, some gathered the eggs; but it was like emptying a lake with a glass. It was easy to rent the farm. I didn't want to sell it because I knew I could do well running it. The thing I wanted most was for Beppe to come back to what he had left; secondly, I knew I was born a peasant and that the land would never let us down; and I knew I had two children.

With a lump in my throat, a small stash of money, and a lot of will, I left for the city. I couldn't work because of the children, so I rented two little rooms and tried to work at home. I did different things—from dressmaking to hairdressing to embroidering numbers on uniforms. I even managed to save a little money.

Ciccio came home after a year and convinced me to place the children with the Sisters while I found work in a restaurant. I made good tips, and after a few months I moved up to cashier. When they finally offered me the position of manager of the restaurant, I found a woman who would come to take care of the children after they got home from the Sisters. That way I could work at night. I was earning a lot of money, but I wasn't happy about being away from the children. I saw them only as they slept. So, when a friend of Ciccio's offered me a job managing the Motel, I accepted.

The children and I moved to the Motel that was on the road that led to Québec City, not far from Montreal. I had the river in front of me again, but this time I was on the other bank and could see the sunrise. I did all the manual labor and Ciccio's friend handled the money. A year later he let me take care of the cash as well, and he would come in once a week to check everything. I hired a woman and a young man for help. In the summer we built other cabins and we were always busy.

Beppe wrote once a week. He was fine, but he wanted to come home.

The winter brought less work and I was able to take care of the children a little more. I even found time to take lessons in Italian,

English and French from a retired professor—
an old, tired and lonely Italian who lived in a
small house near us. He was a very cultured
man who said he knew Matilde of Canossa like
his own mother. I learned from him that it
was the Emperor's son who had died fighting
against our Abbey, and who the Longobardi
were; and he knew that many hundreds of
years ago we had been great heroes, and we
had protected the road to Rome for two hundred years. He taught me many things and
said that with what I had learned I could have
gone to university.

The war got worse and the Motel didn't
have many guests. I laid off the woman and
made do with the young man and myself.
Then the owner got sick and said he wanted to
sell. I asked my tenants on the farm for four
years' rent in advance. I applied for a new
mortgage and bought the Motel.

I was thirty-eight years old. Rosa was seven
and Dino was six. They went to school nearby.
I had heard that Beppe would soon be home.

I owned some land and a Motel, and yet I wasn't completely satisfied. Maybe that's why I always worked so much. I saw every dawn and stayed up with many stars. If I stopped, a deep pain would grip my heart. It was a pain made of many things and nothing. I felt like a stranger to myself, to my children and to the place where we lived. I wasn't satisfied with myself. When I heard that Beppe was coming home I couldn't understand why, after having waited so long, I felt so much anguish.

Ciccio asked me, "Will you come to Montreal to pick him up?"

"I'll wait for him at home," I said.

"I'll bring him to you," said Ciccio. Beppe arrived with Ciccio's whole family.

I had dressed-up myself and the children. I had made *tortellini* and chicken, and offered champagne to everyone. Beppe was in very good health. He was big and strong. He had been a lumberjack in the camp and had eaten well. His hands were cracked and his face was burned from the sun and wind. He was, all in all, just as he had been when he left. I had changed a lot, he told me as he embraced me.

"You seem like a real lady."

I smiled and felt disappointed having dressed myself that way. Everyone was happy, but I couldn't wait for them to leave. Ciccio had drunk too much champagne and said, "See, I gave you a first-class wife. She's turned herself into a millionaire, a millionaire!"

I could feel Beppe's humiliation.

"I am full of debt," I said.

"I'd like to have your debts," someone else said.

"I'll pay them off with Beppe's help," I said again. Everyone left and I told the children to stay with us. I didn't want to be alone with Beppe.

"Let me see your property," said Beppe.

"Our property," I said.

"Thank-you," he said. Then he looked at his hands.

"I must seem like a real peasant to you."

"You are always you, Beppe. And I am always me."

"The children are beautiful," he said. "I recognized them from the pictures. I didn't recognize you."

"You will," I said. I told the children to go to bed, then showed Beppe the Motel. There were no guests that night because of the cold and the snow. Beppe never said a word. When we went back inside and took off our shoes, he simply said, "Good."

We sat in front of the fire, alone and distant from each another, worse than two strangers. We didn't say anything for awhile, then he said, "I wanted you so much when I was at the camp. Now I feel like I don't have the courage to touch you."

Why?"

"Because you're someone else."

"I'm always me." I moved closer to him.

"Touch me, you'll see it's still me." And Beppe started touching me, as if he didn't know me. Then he took me in his arms and carried me up the stairs to the bedroom. I was telling myself, 'Nothing's really changed, really.' Once again I had to try to distance myself from my desire for the earth against my back and the stars in my eyes.

Then Beppe said, "It's true. It's just as if only a few days have passed, not three years."

So again we started working side by side. Beppe worked a lot on the Motel and rebuilt the cabins which were in bad shape. The summer brought many guests. The river was constant; freezing in winter, melting in the spring. We bought more land, built more cabins and a small restaurant adjoining the house.

The war ended. My mother died during a bombing and my father followed her in grief. Torquato ended up in Russia. Edmea still had three children, and a damaged home with the earth dug up from the bombs. I sent money for them to fix the house and straighten out the land. I held on to Torquato's money for his return. The pain inside me was growing stronger. It was the pain of my land.

That winter, we decided to put the children in an excellent private school in Montreal. We now had the means to give them the best education. We took them to school Monday mornings and brought them home Friday afternoons. Apart from a good education, I also wanted them to have good friends for their future, and Beppe agreed that it was better to leave them in town rather than break up our long nights of work.

That Monday, there came a big blizzard and Beppe called to let me know that the roads were terrible and that he was stopping at Ciccio's since he was afraid of being caught in the storm in our little van. "There won't be any work tonight anyway."

"That's for sure." It was a horrible night of snow and wind and there were no cars on the road. Over the radio the police kept telling people to stay put. We certainly wouldn't get

any guests. However, at midnight, while I was
sleeping, I thought I heard the bell ring. I
heard a noise and got out of bed. I called Dick,
the watchman, from the stairs.

"Yeah," he told me, "it's actually a
customer."

"On foot," said the voice of a man.

That voice rang in my thoughts for a
moment and then I put my robe on and went
downstairs. It was Adelmo. We looked at each
other without speaking. Then I looked away
and said to the watchman, "Prepare number
two." Turning back to Adelmo, in French, I
asked, "Would you like something to eat?"

"Yes please," said Adelmo in Italian. My
hands and legs shook as I stepped past him.

"On foot?"

"My car slid into a ditch not far away from
here, fortunately."

'Fortunately?', I asked myself.

"It sank into the snow. I had a hard time
getting out and then I saw the neon sign of the

Motel." The watchman came back in, bringing with him a huge cloud of snow. "What a night!" he said. Then he saw me at the stove. "I'll do that," he said. "No," I said, "I'll do it. Go get some sleep." He didn't argue.

"Steak?" I asked.

"Yes," said Adelmo. I put the steak in the pan and prepared some coffee.

"Climene . . ." said Adelmo.

"My mother and father died," I said.

"Mine too. In a bombing. The land was left to my youngest brother. The house was destroyed. I sent money to have it rebuilt."

"Me too," I said.

"My parents are buried at the Abbey," said Adelmo. "It was during the war and that was the closest cemetery."

"My mother and father are there too," I said. "That is our cemetery."

"I see you're married," said Adelmo. "That's good."

"Yes," I said, "We're doing well."

"Me too. I'm alone. I build houses."

"That earns a good living."

"Yes," he said.

"I have two children," I said.

"I have no children," said Adelmo. "The first one died." I felt a great pain in my heart.

"The steak's burning," said Adelmo. He was right. I took it off the stove right away. I set the table. Adelmo sat. I poured his coffee.

"Sit in front of me," Adelmo said. I sat and we looked at each other. It seemed that the whole room was full of warmth and light. Adelmo looked at my hand resting on the table and I withdrew it onto my lap. I remember all my moves and words and the pain inside me as though I were living them now. Adelmo ate in silence. I got a cup and poured myself some coffee.

"Are you happy?" he asked.

"Yes." I said. "Very."

"I'm happy for you," he said. "I always hoped you were very happy. I was never happy. I'm still not happy even with so much

money I don't know what to do with it. Do
you know what I would like?"

I said nothing because I didn't want him to
speak.

"A good old piece of land." I looked at him.

"How about you?" I kept quiet.

"And do you know what else I would want?
You. A good piece of land from home. And do
you know what I have wanted and will always
want now and forever? You, and you again,
and again you. And those gullies and my bro-
ken shoes from when I was a child in the
country and always you."

"Enough," I said in a low voice, but inside I
was screaming. He drew himself back on the
chair.

"The barnyard, the roosters, the wine
feasts. I would want my parents alive. And yet
. . . " he looked at me, " . . . you seem a little
changed."

"You too," I said.

"Who knows," he said, "if things change us
inside? Do *you* know?"

"I don't know."

"You hated me?"

"No."

"I hated myself. I still hate myself today. It was a big mistake in every way. I thought you would get back home. I wrote to my parents. Why aren't you speaking?"

"I have nothing to say." But I wanted to scream. He finished his coffee in one sip and stood.

"Is your husband here?"

"He's in Montreal, he'll be back tomorrow."

"I'll try not to meet him. If this storm stops and I can get the car out . . ." He looked around and added, "Your husband must be a big man, strong and able."

"Yes," I said.

"Do you love him?"

"Yes."

"You loved me," he said.

"I love my husband very much," I said.

"I'm sorry," he said, "for what I said."

I stood.

"I'll take you to your room," I said. "You don't know which one is number two." I took the keys from the board and threw a shawl over my head. Adelmo opened the door and as the wind carried us back, he grabbed my waist and pushed me ahead. We went on like that, in the wind and snow for those few steps, practically embraced.

"Go back!" he shouted in my ear, squeezing me harder. "You'll catch a cold!"

But I would rather have gone on like that the rest of my life and even died. He took the key and opened the door to the cabin. I turned on the light. We were covered in snow. We looked at each other. "Good night," I said.

"A good piece of land," he said with a smile. I turned and ran back to the house. I remember washing that plate, cup and silverware with love as tears ran down my face.

All night I tossed in bed and the hiss of the wind carried my yearning.

Dawn found me awake polishing the furniture. Outside, the storm had died and the silence had relieved nature's hardship, but not mine. Beppe arrived very early and was surprised to find me up.

"You arrived early!" I said.

"I couldn't stand the thought of your being alone in this storm."

"Thank you," I said.

"The road is almost impossible to drive on. Twice I thought I would end up in the river or in a field."

"We have a guest," I said.

"Really?"

"His car went in the ditch."

"I should say!"

"A person from my land back home" I said.

"What a coincidence!"

"Yes," I said. I poured him some hot coffee. Beppe drank it quickly. I looked at him bewildered. I wanted to shout to him: "Help me!"

"You are the strongest woman I know," Beppe said instead. "Never tired, never!"

"I'm homesick, Beppe," I said softly, on the verge of tears.

"There's nothing like seeing someone from home to get you homesick," said Beppe. "Good, good," he said again, rubbing his hands, "we'll celebrate his visit."

Dick entered. He said there was a lot of snow. "I'll help you," said Beppe. "No," I said. "Stay here. It's early. No one will come today anyway." Beppe was surprised. "Stay here," I repeated. "Dick can shovel to number two by hand. It's early."

"But . . ." said Beppe.

"Then I'll come and help too."

"Well all right," said Beppe. "I'll have another cup of coffee." We had a cup together. I sat very close to him. I remember feeling scared and wanting Beppe to help me make the world disappear.

"Rosa and Dino will have lots of fun with all this snow," he said. And all of a sudden, there it was, between us, the shadow of my other child. I felt I had no strength, I felt like I was at the end.

"What's wrong?" Beppe asked, looking at me.

"Nothing. I must have caught a cold."

"You're shaking all over!"

"It'll pass. It must have been the cold . . ."
The door opened and Dick came inside.

"The guest left," he said. I jumped to my feet.

"He didn't sleep either," he said. "The bed's still made." I fell back down on the chair.

"Strange man," said Beppe.

"He left ten dollars on the table."

"You keep it," I said.

"Thanks!" said Dick.

"I'm going to help Dick," Beppe said, and I didn't stop him. Instead, I wished he would leave as well, in the snow, quietly, like the father of my child had left. I stayed alone in the silence and from the window I could see the blue frozen river and I wanted to slide my way to the middle of it, lie down and end everything.

They found Adelmo in his car in the ditch, he was already cold. I never saw him. Beppe told me about it.

I then found out from Edmea that according to Adelmo's wishes, he had been buried in the Abbey's cemetery near his parents.

"We will come back here to die," Adelmo had said.

*T*EN YEARS passed, during which we saved our fortune. Our farmland was bought for an incredible price following the Sea-Way project. The value of our Motel also increased due to our renovation of older buildings and adding new ones. We were considered well off in Canada, rich in Italy.

We built a bungalow for ourselves with every comfort. The children were grown-up. Rosa was twenty, Dino nineteen. I had a lot of gray hair and had gained weight. I suffered from arthritis, probably from straining myself in the past. Beppe was hunched over a bit and seemed older than he was. He still worked hard, but he had lost some of his sight and hearing as well.

In those ten years we thought of one thing: return to Italy. I held on to that thought like a sickness. We would talk about it, Beppe and I, in the calm evenings. I did most of the talking. Beppe would listen. He sometimes tried to object to this decision, but I would always convince him otherwise. Even the children seemed to side with me. Although they loved their life in Canada, they were convinced by my words. I made plans for their future in Italy. Rosa, who wanted to be a pharmaceutical chemist, would acquire a pharmacy. Dino wanted to be an engineer, and once he finished studying, we would set him up with a construction firm. Beppe and I would relax.

So for ten years we lived for our plans and I think everyone thought it was all a dream, except for me. I didn't know and didn't want to feel what the others were feeling.

We finally decided to make a preliminary trip to scout things out. We couldn't find anyone to take care of the Motel so Beppe would remain. I would go with the children, and then we would come back to sell every-thing and move.

The anticipation of that trip made me very happy. Beppe, instead, was solemn and I thought it was because he couldn't come with us. I tried to console him.

"No," he said, "I'll be even sadder when we leave for good." I looked at him astonished.

"Are you serious?" Beppe looked at me for the first time, I think, with hatred and pity.

"Yes," he said. "I'm very attached to the Motel."

"It has done well for us," I said.

"You see," said Beppe, "I love this Motel as much as I love you. It seems strange to me that you aren't as attached to the thing that you yourself created."

"I *am* attached to it," I said.

"You aren't attached to *anything*," he said. I looked at him horrified. I couldn't believe it was Beppe talking.

"What do you mean?"

"I can't explain myself, and perhaps you wouldn't understand, but sometimes I think you live in a dream you can't wake up from."

"What are you saying? My whole life has been a positive reaction to a series of events. What dream?"

"Yes," said Beppe, "I don't know how to explain myself." I smiled at him.

"Don't wear yourself out." I said jokingly, then a doubt came to my mind, "Do you want to go back to your village?" I asked.

"I could never live there."

"On a hill, far from the city . . . ?" I asked, looking for words, feeling guilty. His village was stranger to me than Canada.

"Yours is also on a hill."

"But the university isn't far," I said.

"It's not *my* village that I was talking about," he said. It's here. This is where we started our life. It's almost as if we were born here. It's not 'my' place or 'your' place. It's 'our' place."

I looked at him with my heart tight, while he turned and slowly went to white-wash the benches along the river. The next day Beppe told me that Rosa and Dino were also attached to Canada.

"The only difference is that they were born here," I said, "but in their souls they are just like you and me." A few days later, at the table with Rosa and Dino, Beppe said, "The misery of selling the Motel will take years off my life."

I didn't get mad. "Do you or *don't* you want to go back to Italy?"

"No," said Beppe decisively, shaking his big head. I reddened with anger.

"And you decide this now?"

"The more I think about it, the more it hurts," he said.

"We've been planning this for ten years," I said.

"The closer we get to leaving, the more it hurts. I'm attached to the Motel, to the people I know, even to the guests I don't know, to the

road, the river . . ." And Beppe's eyes filled
with tears.

"Oh, Daddy!" exclaimed Rosa as she started
to sob.

"So much effort," I said, "ten years of planning, and then this . . ."

"*We* want to go to Italy," said Dino, "but it's
sad too . . ."

"This is our country," Rosa said, drying her
tears. "For us, leaving here is like when you
left there . . ."

"Me?" I looked at each of them one at a
time and felt a great distance—they could
never know. I felt as alone and miserable as I
did when I arrived here and found my life in
pieces. I had picked up those pieces one by one
and put them back together.

"You don't understand us, mother," Dino
said. "We love your country, but we are
Canadian." I was hurting. I suffered because I
felt they were asking me to defend them
against something, but I didn't know what.

"We understand you, mother," said Rosa. "You don't understand us. We don't want to offend you."

"You understand *me*." I stammered. And I looked to Beppe for help, but Beppe held his head low. I had a terrible pain inside me.

"We'll stay," I said. All three of them jumped at me to say I didn't understand, that they were happy to go to school in Italy and establish themselves there, and Beppe would retire.

"We'll try it," I said and felt even lonelier.

"Of course," said Beppe with relief, "we can try it and if we don't like it we can stay here. If we like it, we can go there." And so, they thought they had reassured me and we no longer talked about it. I kept giving them the impression that I was in need of help, but I didn't know why. I didn't know and I couldn't understand—and I was hurting, waiting for something definitive and wrong to happen to them. In the end I was glad that Beppe stayed behind at the Motel. I was as happy as when I had tied up the cows or gathered the chickens in the chicken coop as a child.

W HEN OUR departure day came, no one was exceptionally happy. Many people came to say good-bye with Ciccio and Catina. Everyone cried as if we were leaving for good, and we all kissed as though we were brothers—and Beppe was there in the middle of so many people that were supporting him, and it seemed as though we'd never see each other again. When the ship got underway I stayed above to look around me—thinking about my return after twenty-three years.

I was traveling first class. Back then I was carrying a child to whom I had promised such a return. That child was no longer here. Adelmo was also gone. I was going back to my land. My mother and father were dead. Bruno as well, and Torquato still hadn't come back from Russia. But the land was there, and so was Edmea, faithful and vigilant.

I pulled myself away from my thoughts and went in search of Rosa and Dino. They were in the cabin. Rosa tried to hide her red eyes. Dino drummed his fingers nervously on the dresser. I felt like leaving again. Instead, I tried to feel their suffering and it caused me pain.

"Why are you crying?" I asked Rosa.

"I'm O.K. now. I was thinking about when we'd leave for good."

"Don't think about it because we'll probably never leave for good. It depends on whether you like it, if you feel comfortable. You are grown-up and can choose your own life, but first you have to see and learn—then your choice will be clear and without regret. This has to be a *fun* trip. I won't impose any change on you if you don't want it. Your beginning was here in Canada. Canada is a good homeland and it is a homeland where you were born and where you should stay if you want. So be happy. It's a nice ship, isn't it?"

"Yes, beautiful," Dino said.

"There are many young people your age. Go, I'll take care of the luggage."

Later, I found them on the deck looking at the land beyond the dark waters. I didn't go near them. I was scared, scared of our different feelings, of our different interests. I returned to the cabin and tried to write to Beppe, but I didn't know what to say to him, so I tore up the letter.

For two days we navigated on the St. Lawrence and for two days I watched the riverbanks where I had made my life. And for two days I looked at the green land—so big and beautiful—through a veil of tears. It was an agony I recognized, to abandon and start over, to lose and suffer. It was being and knowing and counting the drops of your own sweat and the tears of your own heart. That land, my children's land, was very dear to me, but my transplanted roots were old and sick.

I hid my pain from my children. I wanted them to still feel sure of me. They soon found friends on the ship and forgot their worries. They were on vacation, they were young and had money and nice clothes. They were what I never was, but they were what I would have wanted to be. I wouldn't destroy them for having created them.

*A*T LE HAVRE we got on our first of many trains. I was worried about the suitcases. In the crowd I became the girl whose father had told her that her suitcase was like her home.

In Paris, the children wanted to tour the city since the train for Italy left only at night. I told them I didn't want to leave the suitcases and that I would wait for them at the train station. I wouldn't hear of putting the suitcases in a locker.

I stayed there the rest of the day, near the suitcases, amidst the bustle and commotion. The hours of waiting, my fatigue and impatience, the children's tardiness—all put me in a state of anxiety and solitude that was familiar. In my anxiety I walked back through my life to my childhood and it seemed as though I had walked a lot in life, and for no purpose. Then I went back to the road ahead of me and found myself there, with the many suitcases that were much nicer than the one I had before, with a purse full of money, two grown and good children, a devoted husband, and a huge scar that tortured me inside.

When Rosa and Dino came running, my heart opened up a little. They took the suitcases, guided me to a taxi—since we had to go to a different station—and all the while they told me about what they had seen and in their excitement it all came out a little in French, a little in English, and a little in Italian. My head felt like a volcano. The children got me settled on the train, filled out customs forms, and all of a sudden I realized I didn't know how to do anything anymore. I was more lost and alone than when I had left Italy many years ago; and the children, instead, were stronger and more capable than at the beginning of the trip.

I lay down, promising to get a hold of myself the following day. I didn't sleep the whole night. The anonymous voice that announced our arrival in Domodossola spoke to my heart and my weary limbs. I rose in a hurry. They were speaking Italian outside. I opened the little window. I looked. Cold mountains enclosed us on every side. When the train left again, I stayed at the window trying to recognize my country, but since I didn't know those mountains, I felt a little dismay. At that point Dino opened the door.

"Here we are in your country, mother!" he shouted merrily.

His words hurt me. Were we not of the same blood?

"Not bad!" yelled Rosa from the corridor. "Look at the lake!"

I looked at Lake Maggiore, which I had never seen before.

"It's very different than our lakes," said Rosa. They started talking about the difference between their lakes and my lakes.

For the first time I wished Beppe were at my side. I now understood what the wise old professor had told me—that we Italians are strangers even among ourselves because we still haven't reached common ground. I was as much a stranger to Beppe's land as I was to Lake Maggiore. 'But', I told myself with anguish, 'I will not be a stranger to my hills, I will recognize my bread, my wine and my sky.'

In Milan, we had a hard time finding our next train. Then they told us that *all* the trains went by my area and I felt very important in front of the children. We decided to take the fastest one. It was called the 'Settebello' and the children were very enthusiastic about it. I was worried about the suitcases that were to be placed in another car; then I was worried about the speed of the train that was made of glass and seemed to be very fragile. My children found Italy to be very modern, contrary to what Beppe and I had told them—that it was very poor and lacking in everything but the sun. I felt proud of this train even if it scared me, so I tried to be carefree.

In Bologna, we decided to take a taxi to my home. At that moment, the world seemed to come to a halt, and it gave me time to savor my endless joy. I saw and recognized the roads, the land, the plants, and even my legs were hurting and tired like when I was a girl. My children spoke with the taxi driver, but I wasn't listening.

"My land! My land!" I was shaking inside and it felt myself crying and laughing at the same time. I got dizzy when I saw the first gullies.

"Everything is so small," said the children. But my heart felt so big.

"America makes everything as big as an elephant," said the taxi driver. I had to give directions how to get to my village. We coasted along the Ghiaia Stream, as parched as thirst. Then, all of a sudden, Paraviere stood out, high and lone against the sky over the valleys.

"You don't want me to go all the way up *there*?" said the taxi driver. "You need a mule, not an engine." The suitcase problem made it worse, but the taxi driver didn't want to discuss it. I thought about Adelmo who had made his way up there on his motorcycle.

We paid the taxi driver and I decided that the children would stay and watch the suitcases while I went ahead to get help.

"You'll tire yourself, mother. Let *us* go."

"I know these roads like I know myself," I said. And I set out, up through the hedges and the vineyards, towards that old house of mine with the wheat waving all around me. I was going and laughing and felt free and alone, my heart was untouchable by anyone but me.

All of a sudden, I was out of breath and I had to sit on a stone warmed by the sun. There I stayed and forgot time. I felt as though I was carrying a child, the one I was carrying when I left that place—that we were one and understood each another. We recognized the stones and the blades of grass, the acacias, the roads that led us far away and those that brought us back home. Adelmo was there with us and we were apart from every other being in the world.

Dino caught up with me very worried. He didn't know why I had sat down and was convinced I was sick. I calmed him down, and was immediately worried about the suitcases.

"Rosa stayed with them," he said. We walked up together. Every once in a while I looked at him and understood and felt that we saw things differently, our hearts felt differently. It was like a knife in my heart. Our love for each another could never make us see eye to eye, because while our blood was the same, the land that was in us and from which we sprang was different.

I understood from his sweat, and from his indifference, that *my* land didn't exist, and I could never create it for him because it is something that you absorb in your first steps, your first smiles, your first cries, with your very life itself.

I realized the my sister Edmea hadn't walked. *I* had walked. She was at peace in her tiresome life. And I wasn't happy on the path I had taken, because I realized I couldn't recognize the things I had left behind. I didn't look the same, but still I tried to see them to no avail. Something had mutated inside me that couldn't be reversed. It was as though I didn't know how to sing anymore, nor cry, nor laugh. I was dead, that was it, like the child I had never known and like Adelmo who truly was dead.

Dino and Rosa amused themselves for awhile, a short while. They couldn't speak our dialect and even their Italian was poor. They were smarter than Edmea's and the neighbors' children. They felt like two fish out of water and they couldn't wait to go to town to visit the university. They appreciated picking so many different types of tasty fruits from the trees that seemed special and marvelous. But they couldn't appreciate the gullies, the tortuous and dusty paths leading to the Church, the primitive bathing, the scarcity of water, the light, and other things that, bit by bit, made me feel guilty for them. They spent some time at the Monteveglio Abbey and wandered around the nearby castles. They wondered why I never spoke of all the history that seemed to surround us.

"If only *we* had a castle like *this*!" they said with enthusiasm upon their return. "You have so many and you don't take care of them. You let them fall to pieces," they said. "And you don't realize what you have."

We didn't know them because they were things born with us. They are old and tired stones. "If they disappeared you'd feel their absence," Dino said. "But since they were given to you, you don't even know their history."

Edmea and I understood that if they disappeared we would be upset. But whoever thought they would disappear? It was like thinking that the gullies could disappear.

"They built them strong in ancient times," I said.

"Those stones say something," said Rosa, "but none of you seem to have ever listened."

Their cousins, Edmea's children, were very irritated by this arrogant talk.

"They are young," I tried to apologize for myself and my children. "They don't understand diplomacy."

"They are like elephants in a china shop," said the old Abbot whom we had gone to visit to ask advice. "After the war, many people were left hurt. Tell them to be prudent."

"Don't say everything that comes to your minds," I told them. But they were born in another world, clear and simple—they were my pride and my despair. The situation between us was getting more difficult. Nevertheless we were kind and courteous among ourselves. We respected each other's distant and strange feelings.

My sister Edmea, her husband, and their children were all Communists. I was so surprised because in Canada and in Italy, when I had lived there, being a Communist was a bad thing. My children were horrified by it as well. Edmea kept going to church with her husband. They explained that they really weren't Communists, but that they had to be because that's how it was in the hills after the war. She also had a sister in Canada and it was known that Canada was capitalist. So I understood why they had to be Communists.

My children couldn't understand it though, and Dino had a discussion with many others and said that it was all a question of ignorance, but he failed to make his point— he was tired of being on that hill. He told everyone they were ignorant and that it was all a mistake. He said that he had never seen as much ignorance as in our hills and he said it with reason, but no one understood him.

"Don't worry about it," said the old Abbot. "They are good children, young, with the fear of God in them and raised in a young town also with the fear of God in it. I wish our children were like that; I have so few of them around me. At the same time, however, your children are ignorant as well. They don't know. They never lived here."

"*You* are ignorant," I told the children. "As much as *they* are, if not more, because you know nothing of this place and of the stones that you admire so. You look at things as though they were framed in a picture and you can't see anything else. To know what they know, our rocks and our people, you have to have lived in the midst of them."

I was very worried after that incident because I felt I was no longer considered a part of the people in the hills, because the flesh of my flesh was made of another marrow.

I made a large offering to the Abbey in memory of my parents, but I told the Abbot not to talk about it so as not to hurt Edmea and he understood completely. The Parish

Priest was very thin. He said no one offered him chickens like they used to. I still remembered how much care we took in feeding the chickens for him.

Even on the hills life had changed. The people were tired of sweating, and many left. Even Edmea's children wanted to leave. No one ploughed with oxen anymore, but instead used tractors, and you could see machinery similar to that in America. The people still hung their laundry out in the sun and that reminded me of my times.

Few still baked bread at home, and no one spun yarn anymore. No one gleaned. And they were all very nervous and edgy. You could see they were well, but no one was as happy as I remembered them. They talked about money and politics all the time. The younger ones often went into town to work. They had nice clothes and wore ties. Adelmo had made an impression in his time, now they were all a little like he was, with cars and motorcycles.

I understood why they weren't happy. I understood that they no longer knew how to live the way they used to and be satisfied with it. I would have liked to have stopped them all to make them understand what they had lost. I, too, was unhappy because I had lost my world and I was convinced that it would be a good thing for my children to return to Canada. They were immigrants in Italy and I didn't want them to know my sorrow. I wished I had one land, just one. One that was always the same, that you never lost, or had to look for again, one that you could always recognize.

So one day I said, "I have seen everything, and we are going back to Canada. We won't sell the Motel and we will stay there forever." They hugged me and tore my tired heart to pieces with their joy. Before we left, I went to the cemetery at the Abbey to see Adelmo. He had a simple grave next to his parents. The flowers had dried up. His brother had used the money he sent him to move to the city and he couldn't come often. I sat next to him and promised him that I, too, would rest there near him and my parents, and that way it wouldn't matter to us if the flowers dried out and no one came to visit.

I knew that Beppe wanted to be buried in his town, which for me was stranger than Montreal. So everyone would return home, and it would be like being young again with Mama and Papa and many things to love.

I felt a love for Adelmo that no one would understand. He was like the land, Adelmo, a land where people lived, but no longer loved; but he and I loved it very much because we knew the price of having lost it. I returned to the field where we had loved each another because we were no longer made of that. We were something much bigger and more beautiful, like a flower in the field or a star in the sky.

WE RETURNED to Canada and Beppe was elated to have us back and to know that we wouldn't be leaving. Even I was happy to have come back to the things I had built, in a good place that held the part of my heart I had taken away from someplace else. I may have been even a little happier because everyone says a trip back home always puts things into their right perspective. Everyone wished me well as though I were getting over a sickness . . .

I confided in Ciccio, "My children are different. They don't know anything about Italy. It was as if we were watching two different movies even though we were right next to each other. Here we look at things the same way. It's a good thing they have here and it's better that they stay."

"Dear Climene," said Ciccio. "I knew it would be like that. I am old and have been here for many years and I have seen many things. I have known many feelings, on my behalf and on behalf of others. I tell you it's a good thing for your children to stay and live here. America is made of our children, children from many countries. They *are* this country. The children won't go back. We and our memories are only fairy tales. They don't know the great pain it gave us to leave. But what can we do? They will never know what we suffered. Climene, you gave them a good country and they will be good citizens. What more do you want?"

"Nothing," I said. "That's all I want for them. I didn't know that before, now I do."

Our lives were back to normal, good, just as God had given them to us. The Motel prospered, the children graduated with honors. Beppe's health started worsening and he couldn't do any heavy work. We didn't have the need to do heavy work anymore anyway. I convinced him to take a trip back to his village and he left with Rosa. When he returned, he

said he felt like a king there and that he had
founded a shelter and named it Rosa of the
Roses after our daughter. They had given him
a knighthood and a large certificate with a seal
that they put in a frame. All his people came
to see it and called him 'Sir' and we felt important. Rosa, however, commented that his village was worse than mine. But she said the
people were nice and not Communists.

Rosa then got married to a Friulian immi-
grant. A good-looking, tall, blonde man who
was a designer at an important Canadian firm.
We gave Rosa a big wedding and a reception at
the Motel with colored balloons in the trees
and a live band. The river reflected all the
lights, and people said it was like being in
Venice. I had never seen Venice, but the moon
was out, and I knew the big river and its sun-
rises and sunsets—and its water had seen so
much of my life—and so I thanked it for being
so beautiful on that festive day.

Even Dino was married soon after to an
Italian-Canadian girl. She was good, capable

and old-fashioned; her parents were not able to do for her what we had done for Rosa, but we were happy anyway. We were serene, with children who were settled and happy, who respected their family and religion. We couldn't ask for more.

Beppe was then confined to his bed and I watched him die a little every day. Rosa helped me take care of him, but then she got pregnant and I was the only one at Beppe's bedside for a long time that seemed a lifetime. Beppe would reminisce over and over again about our path through life together. There was so much pride in his voice and in his eyes as he spoke to me.

"You have been the pillar in my life." But he couldn't tell me that I was like his land, and I felt alone, as I did in my home on the top of that hill.

"You gave me a friendship that was an honor and my strength," he said.

"Beppe, you are too generous. I owe to you my entire good life," I told him.

"You are a respectful couple," Ciccio said. "Respect is the secret to an honorable family."

"You are our example," our children told us.

Beppe and I felt a little like two saints. At night, we would say the Rosary together, which helped us feel very far from the world and very close to God. Beppe was leaving me slowly, but peacefully, as he had lived, and I started to feel old and tired.

We gave him a beautiful funeral. Many people came because many people had cared for him. We had violinists in the church and everyone cried. I cried a lot as well since Beppe had been a good companion and we had forged a long road of work and achievement together.

He wanted to return to Italy, so he was embalmed and I accompanied the body on the airplane—to his village that I was seeing for the first time. There were a few houses on a barren cliff, white from the sun and dust. It was a big event for the town, and there was a second funeral. The crying was much greater than in Montreal, although there wasn't any music. His family had also invited others to come to mourn. Everyone was dressed in black which seemed odd with so much light and sun. I had a constant, long procession of people and children following me, but I couldn't understand their dialect. They gave many meals in my honor and we ate outside on the shaded terraces. There were fresh vegetables and the whole town stayed to watch us—I felt strange and different from them and wished Beppe were there with me.

Before I left, I made a large offering at the shelter that Beppe had founded, and the Sisters organized a feast in my honor with children dressed as angels who sang and gave me a big bouquet of flowers, which I brought to Beppe's grave.

So I said goodbye to Beppe forever and thanked him for the good life he had given me.

I returned to Canada, to the Motel that, by now, Dino was running on his own, and I understood that I was becoming of little use.

Edmea wrote telling me that her two eldest children were married and had moved to the city, and that the youngest had emigrated to France. They were thinking of going to live with one of their children in the city because they were very lonely. They no longer had the strength to work the land, nor did they have the means to hire good help. They could only sell the land. I understood my land was calling me, that I had to return to my roots with my father, my mother, my brothers—and Adelmo. My children worried, but I reassured them. Ciccio and Catina were also very old, surrounded by a long line of descendants, so they understood. I wrote to Edmea to tell her I was coming home and that we would hire the necessary help for the land so that we could stay and be comfortable in our old age.

"God bless you!" she answered. Again I felt a little saintly just as with Beppe, before his death. I thought of Mama then.

TODAY, I sit here on my mountain which is like a window on the valleys and on my life. I am with Edmea and her husband. The other farmers around us moved to the city and all I see is abandoned land and houses with no lights in them. Every morning, when I rise, I expect to see my little brothers leave for school, smell Edmea's bread from the kitchen, and hear the lowing of the cows from the barn.

One of our hands goes to town for provisions twice a week, and works a little in the barn and a little in the vineyard. The chickens race around, and in the evenings I close them up in the coop like I used to and I feel safe and happy, like I used to.

I can't walk that much anymore. I have a bad heart and rheumatism, so I save my strength to go to the cemetery once a month where my parents are, Adelmo and so many others I knew. It's a peaceful place, full of sun, surrounded by cherry trees. I stay there the whole day to pay my respects to everyone. I'm sorry that Torquato isn't there; he was buried somewhere in Russia. Everyone else is there. Every now and then, someone new arrives and it's rare that I don't know them.

So, bit by bit, we have all come together again, like when we were children, and I am happy to know that I won't grow anymore and I won't have to take on the world anymore, abandoning things and reclaiming them. In the evening, I return home following the crests of the gullies, and I watch the sky change like it used to—while the sun sets and I feel as if I'm on top of the world.

My children worry and want me to come home to them. Dino even came to visit me to try to convince me to go home. He said the

Motel had gotten even larger and that Rosa and her husband joined him as partners which made me very happy because they will be able to walk together in life, and their children will walk together, and that place will be the dearest and most beautiful place in the world to them. I told Dino I was very proud of him. They had planted their feet firmly and found themselves a bench on which to rest.

I couldn't return. My bench was here and that was final. Our house on the hill became beautiful, even Dino admitted it. We can change many things with money. What we can't change is our substance. But he had no idea what I was talking about.

So Dino left. Then Rosa came to visit me. I am serene and at peace even if no one except for Edmea and her husband understands me. Especially here . . . because here the people can't understand, while in Canada all the immigrants understand and can read your heart because they have been through it and they know. What they don't know is how to return and relive their childhood, through their own people who have passed away, on their own land. But I know, and have started recognizing all the things around me again. Everything I touch, every flower I pick, every star I see, every scent I smell. I recognize the sunsets and the thunder storms, the wind and the dew, the familiar lowing of the cows, and the distant barking of dogs.

I feel as if I am already dead and happy. My scar doesn't pain me anymore. People say I'm a little crazy, that my arteries have hardened, and that with my money I could live in a nicer place. I have seen little, even if I have walked much; and beyond this hill there is my little corner in Canada, and the world seems huge already with just these two places.

Here I am alone and free, like a swallow, even if I can't walk very well. I have the sky and the land in my eyes and in my heart, and there is nothing else I need because I have finished walking, and everything is becoming smaller and smaller with every day on this earth. Only the sky stays big, immense, like that night, under the stars, when Adelmo and I decided on our future and created our child, and it seemed that the world wasn't big enough for my heart, only the sky.

The sky.

A NOTE ON THE TYPE

The text was set in 14 point Spectrum with a leading of 18 points space. Jan Van Krimpen designed Spectrum for the Dutch Enschedé foundry in 1952. Spectrum is a direct descendant of the great Aldine types of Venice, which are characterized by their pen-based curves and oblique serifs. As venerable as its forebearers are, Spectrum has a crisp twentieth-century feel.

~

The display font, Cochin, was initially released by the Paris foundry Deberny & Peignot in 1912. Also known as Sonderdruck, Cochin was adapted by many other foundries in the 1920s. The version used for this novel was created in 1977 by Matthew Carter for Linotype. Cochin, named for the nineteenth-century printer Nicolas Cochin, has a small x-height with long ascenders and several unusual letter shapes, notably in the lowercase italic.

Composed by Charles B. Hames
New York, New York

Printed and bound by
Haddon Craftsmen